Why Snails Have Shells

MINORITY AND HAN FOLKTALES FROM CHINA

Retold by Carolyn Han

Translated by Jay Han

Illustrated by Li Ji

A KOLOWALU BOOK

University of Hawaii Press

Honolulu

Dedication

To the people who have passed oral traditions down from generation to generation, and to those who took the time to write their stories in the many languages.

To my students in China, and especially to the minority students at Yunnan Institute of the Nationalities, who had so much more to give than I had to teach.

To my parents and family, who have loved me. To my friends, who have encouraged me. And to David, my son, who is my connection with China.

Library of Congress Catalog Card Number 93–25769
ISBN 0–8248–1505–X
Printed in Singapore
93 94 95 96 97 98   5 4 3 2 1

Designed by Paula Newcomb

University of Hawaii Press books are printed on acid-free paper
and meet the guidelines for permanence and durability
of the Council on Library Resources.

Contents

Introduction

MY INTEREST IN CHINESE MINORITY FOLKTALES began in 1985, while I was teaching English in China at Chongqing University in Sichuan Province. At the end of my first year in China, I wanted to know more about minority people and moved "South of the Clouds," as Yunnan Province is known in Chinese.

For the next two years I lived and worked in the capital city of Kunming. Teaching English at Yunnan Institute of the Nationalities allowed me daily contact with students from the twenty-two different ethnic groups that inhabit this remote southwestern section of China.

On any day in the downtown streets of Kunming you can expect to see Yao, Yi, Miao, Zhuang, Tibetan, Hani, Dai, Naxi, and many other minority people clothed in colorful native dress. They create quite a contrast with the Han Chinese, who often wear drab blue and green.

Surprisingly, my minority students did not wear their traditional clothing or seem to relate to their varied ethnic identities. I soon gathered that minority people were treated differently from the Han and that my students wanted to blend in with the larger group. In class I tried to encourage the students to share stories and poetry from their varied cultures. We all began to learn from the multiplicity of cultures within our group. Many of the students then wanted to know more about their roots, and a sense of pride began to develop. My collection of folktales started with my students. As is usual with teaching, I always learn more than I ever teach.

When I returned to Hawaii, I wanted to share these delightful and informative stories with American readers to promote a greater cultural consciousness and a broader world view.

The collected tales needed to be translated into English. Because my skills in Chinese are limited, I asked Jay Han, a native of Yunnan, for assistance. He helped select the stories for this collection and explained the difficult-to-understand cultural nuances of the tales. He also wrote the Chinese characters on p. 60.

Artwork is visually important to make the tales come alive. The Yunnan artist Li Ji, with his love for animals and our environment, and his deep understanding of the ethnic minorities, has given life to the book.

Many of the tales in this collection teach moral or cautionary lessons. Some resemble the famous *Jataka Tales* that Gautama Buddha used during his lifetime for instruction in India. Many more have food as a main theme. In China, where the common greeting is "Have you eaten?" it is no wonder. Other stories explain how things in nature have come about. I hope this collection of tales will delight and entertain, and that it will make your life richer as it provides new insights into China and its people.

These tales also offered an explanation to give my son when he asked, "Mommy, why do snails have shells?" I had an answer, and you will too.

Why Snails Have Shells

— ZHUANG TALE —

IN ancient times long forgotten, the snail led a very active life. She moved quickly and freely because she didn't have a heavy shell to restrict her movements.

One day, as the creatures worked in the rice fields, the sky turned the color of slate, and thunder roared in the distant mountains. The creatures stopped eating to look up toward the heavens, and they saw the black rain beating its way in their direction. Before long, rushing torrents of mud were everywhere. The horrified creatures ran in all directions to search for shelter.

The snail, being the fastest, soon found a spiral-shaped shell and jumped inside for protection. Immediately she felt snug and comfortable inside the cozy shell, and she fell fast asleep.

Flap-flap-flap, a sound interrupted her dreams. "Please, please let me in," pleaded a dragonfly. "The rain is tearing holes in my delicate wings."

"What do I care?" answered the snail harshly. "Don't bother me. Go away."

Later, a persistent scratch-scratch-scratch again woke the snail. "Please let me in," cried a tiny voice. "I am terrified of being washed away."

This time the snail's voice was filled with outrage: "This is my house, and ants are not welcome!"

"You don't understand. The water is getting higher, and I don't know how to swim." The ant's plea rose and fell with the fury of the stream but was soon silenced.

Next came a bee, and then a butterfly, but they too received heartless replies.

After two days the raging storm ceased, and the snail awoke to a world filled with sunshine. "Even with all those interruptions I have slept well," she murmured to herself. "But now I'm starving."

She left her temporary protection in search of food. But when she was only a few feet away, she turned back and saw that the pink shell had been polished to a rosy hue by the rain, and the spirals were gleaming like golden rings in the glittering sunlight. "What a beautiful house!" she said out loud. "No wonder the others wanted to share it."

She continued a few more feet and suddenly thought to herself, "If I leave my house, someone will come to take it while I'm away. I just can't take the chance," she decided. "I'll have to carry it with me." With that she began to drag her shell.

Day after day, month after month, and year after year, she carried her shell house with her until she and her house grew together to become one. That is why we still use the term "snail-paced" to mean slow-moving. Ever so slowly she moves through the world.

The Ant and the Anteater

— YAO TALE —

ONE day a little ant was searching the forest for something to eat. He couldn't remember ever being this hungry. He walked and walked until he came upon an animal he had not seen before. This new creature politely asked, "What are you doing?"

The little ant told the creature he was starving and trying to find some food. "Little brother," said the anteater, "my tongue is sweeter than any honey you have ever tasted."

Seeing this new creature with its long snout and its thin, ever so long tongue darting in and out of its mouth made the ant step backward in fear.

The anteater offered again: "I will not charge you. Please have a sample."

At first the small ant hesitated. Then slowly he overcame his fear and climbed right onto the long, sticky tongue. "Well, it really does taste sweet," he shouted as he began to eat. "Just like honey."

After a satisfying meal, the ant asked: "Big brother, I have filled my stomach, but I have many hungry brothers at home. May they come too?"

"Of course. I would like to give all your brothers a treat," smiled the anteater.

When the ant returned home, he told his brothers the good news and they shouted in agreement, "Let's not wait! Let's go now!"

It was easy to find the anteater. He was waiting close to the spot where the ant had left him. Upon seeing his long, glistening tongue swinging from side to side, the brothers pushed and shoved to be first.

4

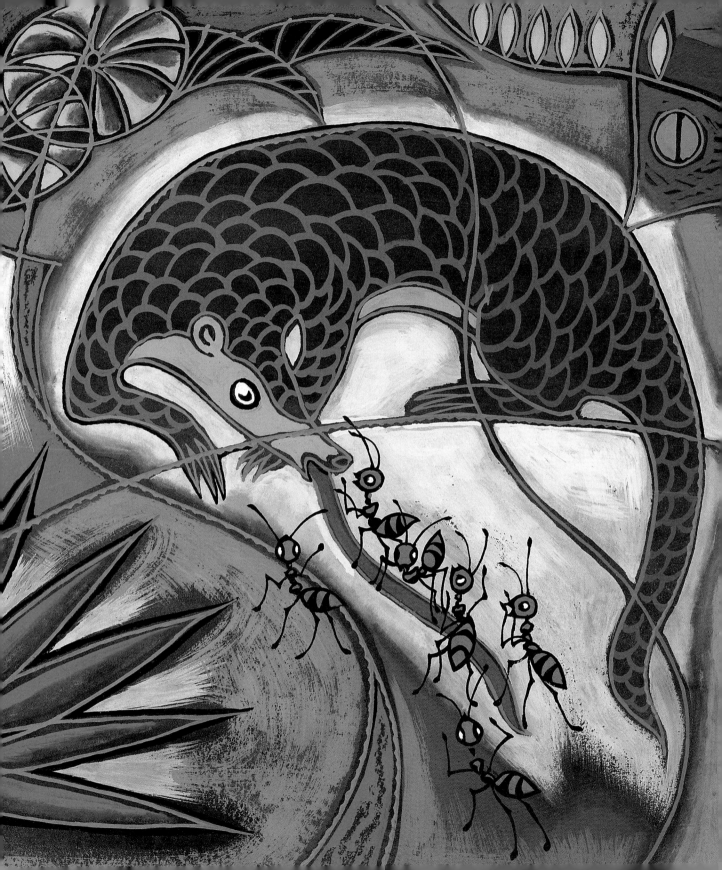

Patiently the anteater waited until all of the ants had climbed onto his tongue. With one big gulp the anteater sucked in his long, sticky tongue. Those in his stomach instantly realized they had been fooled. Those who had yet to meet the anteater would not be able to recognize his face. Even now the shrewd anteater is still getting meals in this way.

The Magpie as Teacher

— YAO TALE —

EVERYONE living in the forest knows that magpies build the most beautiful and the strongest of nests.

A long, long time ago, high up in the tallest mountains along the Li River stood a forest. One day many birds in this forest gathered together to ask the magpie for advice on how to build a nest.

The diligent magpie agreed to show the others. "The most important part of building a nest," she began, "is patience. With patience you can do anything."

All the birds collected around and listened and watched quietly as she picked up a mound of mud and pressed it together to form what looked like a big fat pancake. The magpie patted it carefully, and then she proceeded to make a depression in the middle.

Before she could continue, a thrush suddenly cried, "I know how to build a nest. I never thought it would be so easy." With that the thrush flew to a neighboring tree and began making a nest with mud exactly as the magpie had done. But when it was complete, it looked very ugly.

Unruffled by the thrush, the magpie kept working on her nest. Next she wove small twigs around the edge. As she tucked in the last tendril, a black crow blared out, "Now I know how to build a nest." Away he flew to build his own. When the birds looked up, indeed his had been built of mud and small branches placed on the edge, but the nest was rough-looking with twigs poking out in every direction.

The magpie patiently continued. She brought more mud and put it over the twigs and pressed it down with her beak to make a smooth rim. After

that she placed grass clippings over the mud. Just as she tapped the final piece of grass into place, to form what appeared to be a velvet green carpet, there was a shriek from the sparrow.

"I've learned how! I've learned how!" shouted the sparrow. Soon the birds looked up to see the sparrow in a nearby tree putting together a nest of grass. But it looked crude and unstable.

Finally, the magpie found some fluffy moss, and then she pulled soft, downy feathers from her underbelly. Carefully she placed these in the nest and said, "Now it is complete."

The eagle and the swallow were the only two birds left to hear her words. They had watched the entire time and agreed that it was an amazing nest.

Even though the eagle had stayed for the whole procedure and remembered the complete process, he was just too lazy to try. That is why to this day eagles do not build nests in trees.

Only the swallow listened, watched, and put into practice the lessons of the magpie. Including the most important one—the lesson of patience.

The Flying Frog

— MONGOL TALE —

ONCE long, long ago on the far northern border of Mongolia, there lived an unlikely trio: a friendly frog and a pair of wild geese. They had become the best of friends while sharing the lake.

One summer their lives were turned upside down because of a terrible drought. The water in the lake began to dry up, and soon only a small puddle remained. The geese talked about looking for a new home, but they didn't want to leave without the frog. "Oh, what should we do?" they moaned.

The frog hopped and thought and hopped again. "I have a plan," he said.

He searched around the lake and found a small stick. "It's just the right size," he told the geese. "I'll hold on to the middle of the stick with my mouth, and you can each grab an end. That way you can carry me with you."

"Let's begin the journey today!" shouted the geese.

They flew low over a meadow and spotted a yurt nestled close to a brook. All of a sudden two children appeared from the flap in the yurt, screaming, "Look, look! The wild geese are carrying a frog. What a wonderful idea!"

The frog was glad because it had been his idea. "Yes," he thought to himself, "it is wonderful."

Along the way they flew over a mountain village with many yurts dotting the landscape, and this time dozens of people yelled, "The geese are carrying a frog. What a marvelous idea!"

"This is my idea," the frog almost cried out.

10

They flew onward until they came to a large town. Now hundreds of people came out to watch the frog fly through the air. Cheers came from the crowds below.

The frog couldn't keep his mouth shut any longer. He began to shout, "It's my idea." With the words barely out of his mouth, he fell from the sky, struck the ground, and instantly turned to dust.

The pair of wild geese flew sadly away.

A Fox and a Rabbit

— MONGOL TALE —

A long time ago in the middle of winter, a scrawny red fox trudged through the frozen snow looking for food. As he wandered among the snowy drifts, he came upon an equally thin rabbit. "I haven't had anything to eat for seven days," he complained bitterly.

The rabbit answered in a staccato voice, "Everything is covered with ice and snow. I too have not eaten for days. If my mouth could reach my ears, I might eat them to quell my hunger!"

While they were talking, along came a peasant girl carrying a wicker basket. As she got closer, they both inhaled the sweet aroma of its contents. It was overpowering. "That has to be freshly fried rice cakes," whispered the fox.

"If only we could have a small bite," sighed the rabbit.

"Better than that, we can have them all, Mr. Rabbit," replied the fox. "I have an idea." He told the rabbit his idea, and the rabbit's ears flapped in agreement.

Without being seen, the rabbit quickly ran ahead of the girl. He lay directly in her path pretending to be dead. When she saw what she thought to be a dead rabbit in the snow, she immediately dropped her basket to pick him up. "My family will be so pleased with a delicious rabbit dinner," she said to herself.

The fox, watching from behind a tree, grabbed the basket without hesitation and ran off. The rabbit jumped out of the girl's arms and followed the fox.

The fox ran and ran and ran and ran. As the rabbit chased after the fox,

he soon realized that the fox had no intention of sharing the cakes. Finally, the rabbit caught up with the fox by the side of a small, babbling stream. The fox was holding the largest cake up to his mouth ready to take his first bite.

"Mr. Fox, you are very foolish," chided the rabbit. "If you ate that cake with a fish, it would taste even better."

"I'm sure it would," replied the fox, "but I don't have any fish."

"If you place your tail in the shallow part of the stream, you could easily catch some," suggested the rabbit.

"Why that's a good idea," he said, and he promptly cast his tail into the water. Within seconds his furry tail was frozen firmly in the stream. He couldn't move no matter how hard he tried. All he could do was cry out, "Help! Help! Help!"

The smug rabbit sat down and ate all the fried cakes. When he was finished, he brushed the crumbs off his paws and turned to the fox: "Be patient my friend. Spring will come soon. I'm sure then you'll catch lots of fish."

The Rooster and the Nine Suns

— HANI TALE —

WHEN the world was young, nine suns lived in the sky. The blazing heat from the nine suns began to scorch the earth's surface. Soon the earth resembled a piece of red-hot iron. Nothing would grow, and people began to die.

Groups assembled and discussed ways to save the earth. One person suggested that they find something to cover up the suns with. They thought, but nobody could come up with anything large enough.

Another proposed that the people all hide in caves to avoid the scorching rays of the suns' heat. They tried this for a short time and the caves did give them protection, but they began to starve because nothing grew in the fields. Now people were dying of hunger instead of heat.

Finally, they decided to call upon Erpupolo for help. Everyone knew that he was an excellent archer. Some said he was the best in the world. They would ask him to shoot down the suns with his mighty bow. Erpupolo lived in a cave near Yunjinghong. When they found him they told him about their idea. He listened to the plan and he promised to help.

The next morning before sunrise Erpupolo climbed to the top of the highest mountain. As each sun appeared he loaded an arrow and one by one he shot the suns with his bow. With each pull the bow changed shape from a half moon into a full moon. Eight arrows released, eight suns shot down.

Before he could release the ninth arrow the only remaining sun was so frightened by seeing the other suns shot down that he hid behind a mountain and would not come out.

16

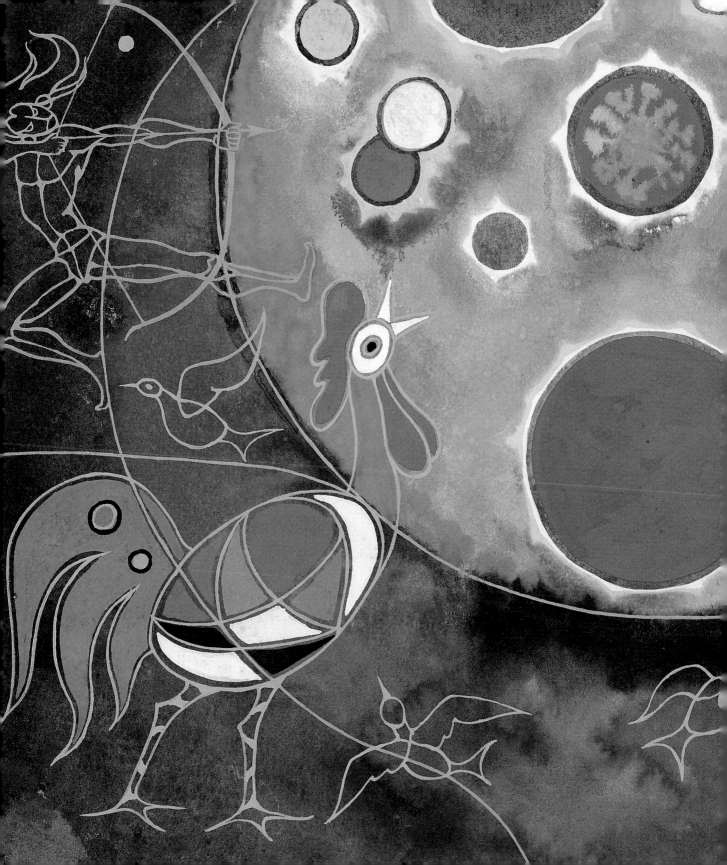

While the people were celebrating the victory, darkness enveloped the earth. Soon the world became desolate and cold. The people realized that they couldn't live without a sun. Without sunshine nothing would grow—nobody would survive. The people tried to call out the hiding sun, but no matter what they said he wouldn't appear. "Who can we get to coax out the sun?" they asked.

Someone suggested the oriole because she is the best singer in the world. The bird was so delighted to be considered the best singer that she promised to help. She began her melodious song, and sang and sang. No matter how beautifully she sang, the sun stayed in hiding.

Then the people asked the skylark. But the same thing happened.

The thrush was the next bird to be asked, but she could not make the sun come out either.

"What about the rooster?" someone asked.

"The rooster doesn't have a beautiful voice," several replied.

"Maybe his voice isn't as lovely as the oriole's, but it is loud, and he is brave and diligent," said another.

When the people asked the rooster, he was glad to help. He stood on his tippy-toes, flapped his wings, stretched his long neck, and began to crow.

The sun heard the rooster's crowing, and even though it was friendly and full of sincerity, the sun stayed hidden.

Again the rooster crowed. This time the sun was deeply touched, but he remained hidden because he was still afraid.

As the rooster crowed for the third time, the sun was sure that he would not be harmed. Since there was no danger, he came out from behind the mountain and showed his full brilliance.

The world turned bright and warm. And from that day until this very morning, as the rooster finishes crowing for the third time, the sun appears in the eastern sky.

The Wolf, the Fox, and the Rabbit

— SALA (SALAR) TALE —

MANY, many years ago in a far-off corner of China, the wolf, the fox, and the rabbit were the best of friends. One day as they were sitting in front of a yurt chatting and drinking green tea, they spotted a peddler off in the distance. The threadbare peddler was balancing a heavy load on a shoulder pole as he made his way down a rocky mountain path.

All at once the three had the same idea. In unison they asked, "How can we separate the peddler from his pack?"

Instantly they knew what to do. The fox and the wolf hid while the rabbit waited in the thicket alongside the path that the peddler would have to take. When the peddler came close to the clump of bushes, the rabbit jumped out singing, "The hills are covered with flowers and the pheasants are flying to and fro." The hungry peddler quickly put down his load in order to catch a meal.

The rabbit led the peddler on a chase, but the rabbit was extremely fast and eventually fled from sight.

When the peddler gave up and returned to where he had left his belongings, they were gone. While the peddler chased the rabbit, the fox and the wolf had stolen the pack and taken it to the wolf's den.

As they entered the den, the fox spoke: "Brother Wolf, I have carried the load all the way, but because you are older and deserve respect, you should have half of it."

At that very moment the wolf realized that the fox did not intend to share with the rabbit. Now this gave the wolf an excuse to keep the pack

for himself. "Why should I share with such a black-hearted fox," he thought, "now that I see his evil side?"

"If I don't kill you now, I'll die at your hand," shouted the wolf. As this curse left the wolf's mouth, he jumped on the unsuspecting fox. With one deadly bite, the fox lay lifeless.

When the rabbit reached the wolf's den, he saw the fox lying in a pool of blood. Trying to hide his fear, he said: "Dear Brother Wolf, I am honored to have your friendship. That's enough for me. I don't want the peddler's belongings."

The wolf had planned on eating the rabbit, but after hearing such kind words, he changed his mind. "Rabbit, watch over my things while I nap. I'm very tired." He yawned as he spoke.

While the wolf was sleeping, the rabbit rummaged cautiously through the peddler's things and found a package of sugar. Silently he opened the brown wrapper, and he immediately had an idea.

"Aiya! This is so delicious," the rabbit said in a loud voice. "Why, I have never tasted anything more delectable," he added, closing one of his eyes.

"What's so delicious?" the wolf demanded.

The rabbit quickly answered, "I have just eaten one of my eyeballs and found it to be the most luscious morsel."

The wolf believed the rabbit's story. "Hurry," he told the rabbit. "Dig out both my eyes. I also want this succulent snack." The wolf's eyes were quickly dug out and dipped into sugar, and then they were eaten by the greedy wolf.

"You are right. They are very sweet and tasty," agreed the wolf. "But now I'm blind."

"Oh, that's easy to cure," the rabbit assured him. "I'll take you to the magic spring high up by the waterfall. After you drink the enchanted water, you'll be able to see again," he promised.

The rabbit led the blind wolf high up the craggy mountain to a cliff ten thousand feet high and said, "Step a little to the right." As he stepped closer to the edge, he lost his balance and fell to his death.

"Greedy wolf," the rabbit laughed loudly, "you deserved to die."

The rabbit returned to the den and started sorting through the packages. He came across one that looked very similar to the package of sugar, but it was wrapped in green paper. "I'll have just a little taste," he said, and he proceeded to put his finger in the white powder and then into his mouth. He realized too late what he had eaten. "Someone help me!" he screamed. "I've been tricked. It isn't sugar—it's poison!" Death came promptly.

Early the next day the empty-handed peddler was returning to his village and passed the wolf's den. Seeing his opened package of poison laying at the entrance, he lowered himself into the small opening in the cliff and crawled inside. His parcels were scattered all about. Quickly he tied them to his shoulder pole: "Yesterday I felt like the most unfortunate fellow, but today all that has changed. Not only do I have my belongings, but I also have two beautiful fur pelts to carry home. Out of what we call dark often comes light," he exclaimed, as he hoisted the pole onto his shoulder.

The peddler never knew the story of the greedy wolf, the cunning fox, and the conspiring rabbit, and how they betrayed their friendships and lost their lives.

A Vain Raven

— TIBETAN TALE —

ONCE, long ago a hungry fox was lounging in the warm autumn sun thinking of the tastiest things to eat. "If only I could catch a raven," he thought to himself. Almost by magic he saw a raven flying in the distance. "If I lie down and pretend to be dead, the raven will come to have a taste of my meat," he said. "As soon as she comes close, I'll. . . ."

The fox lay down in an open meadow so that he could be easily seen. Soon the raven was flying overhead, but when she came close to the fox, she sensed that something was wrong and promptly flew away.

The fox realized that the raven was smarter than he had anticipated. He would have to try another way.

One afternoon a few days later, he saw the same raven flying toward him. He called to the bird with the greatest respect: "Dear Miss Raven, I have not seen you for a long time. After each meeting I cannot get over your ever-increasing beauty. The ebony hue of your lustrous feathers gleams in the sunlight. The golden brightness that shines from your fiery eyes puts the stars to shame. The symmetry of your sleek body can only be compared to a porcelain statue. But most lovely is the elegant way you walk; you carry yourself just like a princess."

The raven cocked her head and listened intently. She was so delighted to be told such flattering things that she flew down from the sky and stood quite near the fox. She began preening her glossy feathers while walking back and forth in front of her admirer.

The raven's chest swelled as she continued to parade. All the while the cunning fox pretended to have great concern for her. "Miss Raven, your

silky cloak of feathers is ever so beautiful but I fear not thick enough for winter. How do you manage in the coldest season?"

"Please don't worry, Mr. Fox," the raven assured him. "When the days become shorter, I go to bed earlier. I can bury my head under my wing, and that protects me."

"You are not only beautiful but also very clever." The fox's voice filled with admiration. "But I don't understand. How can you manage to bury your head under your wing?"

"Oh that's easy," boasted the raven. "I'll show you."

With that the proud raven buried her head deeply under her wing.

The clever fox took this opportunity to have his long-awaited meal.

Two Quarrelsome Cats

— TIBETAN TALE —

ONCE upon a time in a long forgotten forest, there lived two cats who were brothers. The older brother was black as onyx, and the younger one was orange as amber. Each day the brothers worked long hours building their house, and because of their hard work the house was completed in a very short time. Only one thing was left to finish and that was the door.

As they fastened the hinges to the door and put the final touches on their home, the younger one said, "Black brother, let me move in to the house first."

"We built the house together," shouted the black cat. "Why do you want to move in first?"

Their quarreling became louder, and a passing fox stopped to listen. Finally the fox said, "Stop your fighting. A problem has many solutions. I can help. It's easy." With a flash he was gone. The brothers waited patiently for his return.

Soon the fox came back with a blazing torch in his hand. Quickly he set fire to the roof and then to the newly made door. As the brothers watched their house burn to the ground, they realized the fox had tricked them and that they had been foolish to quarrel in the first place.

Strolling hand-in-hand, they both agreed that they had lost their house but learned a valuable lesson. They continued their walk through the sunny part of the forest and soon came upon a small store that sold sweet rice cakes. Feeling hungry, they bought a cake. The orange cat divided it

into two pieces. But one piece was a little larger than the other. At once they began to quarrel.

"Your piece is bigger than mine," wailed the black cat. "No it isn't. They are the same," screeched the orange cat. A nearby monkey heard their argument and tried to stop them: "Don't quarrel. Please don't quarrel. May I help you to divide the pieces evenly? I guarantee they will be the same size."

The brothers handed the two halves to the monkey. The monkey took one bite from the larger piece and compared the pieces again. Then he took a bite from the other one. The monkey continued taking bites until only two tiny pieces were left. "Now they are equal," he said as he handed them back.

The unsmiling cats stood holding their wee pieces of cake and looked at each other, knowing that they had once again been outsmarted and had lost because of their quarreling.

The Rabbit Judge

— TIBETAN TALE —

ONCE upon a time in a faraway land to the north of present-day China, there was a hungry wolf who searched the woods to find food. Unfortunately, instead of finding something to eat, he found a trap set by a hunter and fell to the bottom. Try as he might, he could not free himself.

Soon a goat came along and heard the pleading cries of the captured wolf. "Help, help! Please save me!" came a voice from the deep pit. "I have three children at home. If I die, they will perish," continued the cries.

Standing on the edge of the hole, the goat shook her head and said, "No, no, I can't save you. If I do, you will eat me."

"I swear if you help me, I will never touch a hair on your body," promised the wolf.

The good goat was convinced and hurried off to find a rope. She tied one end of the rope to her horn and threw the other end to the wolf. The wolf grabbed fast to the rope, and soon the goat pulled him to freedom.

As soon as the wolf was freed, he said to the goat, "My sister you were foolish to set me free. Now be foolish enough to let me eat you."

"But you swore you would not harm me," exclaimed the goat.

"I am hungry," snarled the wolf. "I was born to eat meat."

Just then along came a rabbit. The goat told the rabbit the story and begged the rabbit to decide what was fair.

After listening to the goat's side of the story, the rabbit said, "I can't decide by listening only to your account of what happened. I also need to hear from the wolf."

29

At once the wolf began telling his side while the rabbit patiently listened. When the wolf finished, the rabbit spoke slowly: "You both have good points, but if you show me what actually happened, I will be better able to make a decision."

The wolf thought to himself, "The goat cannot run away. I might as well show the rabbit what happened." And with that he jumped back into the trap and waited for the goat to throw him the rope.

The goat began to tie the rope to her horn, but before it could be tossed into the pit, the rabbit grabbed the end.

"Wolf," shouted the rabbit, "this good goat would have saved your life. But being the ungrateful fellow that you are, you will have to wait for the hunter."

"Please help me! I will not break my promise again," cried the wolf. His cries grew fainter and fainter to their ears as the goat and rabbit strolled down the path and out of the woods.

The Monkey's Experience

— HAN TALE —

ONE warm summer morning a long, long time ago a monkey went to town to buy a new set of china. The dishes were such a bargain that she bought more than she could carry in her hands. "How will I manage all this?" she said to herself.

That instant she glanced out of the double wooden doors of the shop and saw a woman walking in the alley carrying vegetables in her bamboo basket. "That's a great idea," she said, and she went directly to the bamboo shop to buy a basket.

On the way home the happy monkey began to sing because she was very pleased with her purchases and proud of her cleverness. Her song grew loud as she approached her home:

> *I am so smart*
> *I'm a world apart*
> *from all the other*
> *monkeys!*

A few days later the monkey's house caught fire. At once she threw the basket to her son and told him to fetch water from the river to put out the fire.

She waited and waited, but her son did not return. Finally, she ran to the river to see what had happened. She found him standing knee-deep in the water dipping the basket in the river and then watching the water flow

32

back out the bottom. When he saw his mother, he turned toward her: "Mother, I have tried, but the basket will not hold the water," he wailed.

"You are such a fool!" she scolded. "Didn't you see me the other day carrying all the china?"

She grabbed the basket from her son and began to scoop the water. Try as she might, the basket would not fill. "It is still empty!" she shouted. "You have ruined my basket."

A Tiger and His Master

— HAN TALE —

AGES ago in the remote mountains of China, there lived a huge tiger. This giant striped beast was so clumsy and slow that he couldn't catch enough food to eat no matter how hard he tried. He was always hungry.

One day while the tiger searched for food, he saw a black cat skipping through the forest. As the tiger watched, his heart beat in rhythm with the cat's lively movements. "If only I could be like him," he sighed.

Late that afternoon the tiger happened upon the same cat leaping from rock to rock in order to cross a river. Amazed by his agility, the tiger could not keep silent: "Please, Master Cat, please teach me your secrets."

The cat balanced on two of the slippery stones and shook his head from side to side saying, "No, no. If I teach you all I know, someday you might turn on me."

"I would never! Why would I hurt my teacher? You would be as respected as my own parents," he pleaded.

The cat saw tears in the tiger's downcast eyes, and because cats have tender hearts, he said, "Well, if you will really keep your promise, I can teach you."

The happy tiger kowtowed before the cat and swore, "From this day on, if I do anything wrong to my master, let me fall down a ten-thousand-foot cliff and break into a thousand pieces."

They began the lessons. Day and night the tiger studied and learned from his careful and patient teacher. Many months passed. One day while in class the cat realized that the tiger was looking at him in a new and

strange way. More important, he noticed that the tiger's mouth was watering. Saliva dripped from the furry muzzle. Instantly the cat knew what was in the tiger's mind, and he stopped the lesson. "I have taught you all I know," he said. "From this day on, you are on your own."

At first the tiger did not believe his teacher's words, and he asked, "Master, did you really teach me everything you know?"

The cat as black as ink replied in a solemn voice, "Yes, my student, I have taught you all I can."

Suddenly the tiger shouted to his teacher, "Master look, look in that tree!"

As the cat turned to look at the tree, the tiger lunged. But the tiger was not quick enough, because in a split second the cat had climbed to the very top.

The cat's smile was gone as he looked down from the tree. "Today my heart is heavy," he said. "Not only are you ungrateful, you have betrayed your word. I had one last thing left to teach you, but had I taught you the final lesson, I would have been your meal.

And now you know why, still to this day, tigers cannot climb trees.

The Corn-Picking Monkey

— HAN TALE —

ON a misty morning long ago on Emei Mountain in Sichuan, a monkey saw a cornfield in the hazy distance. He followed the path along the slippery stone steps until he was standing directly in front of the biggest golden ear of corn that he had ever seen. He reached up and picked it. Balancing the heavy load on his right shoulder, he started for home.

A little further on the path, the monkey passed by a splendid peach orchard. Seeing the biggest, ripest, juiciest peaches made him put down the golden ear of corn and select two delectable pieces of fruit. One for each hand.

As he made his way carefully down the near-vertical stone steps, he came upon a field of watermelons. The sight of the green and yellow striped fruit made his mouth water. He forgot all about the peaches and jumped into the leafy patch and began thumping watermelons. He thumped and thumped and finally he found the one he wanted and hoisted it on his back to carry home.

With such a heavy load he walked slowly along the wooded portion of the mountain. All of a sudden a rabbit ran out from behind a slender tree and sat in the clearing. The monkey tossed his watermelon on the ground in order to chase the rabbit.

He chased and he chased until the rabbit disappeared down the side of a craggy cliff. Now he was very far from where he had left his watermelon, and he couldn't remember the way back.

At the end of a long day the monkey had no corn, no peaches, no watermelon, and no rabbit. Empty-handed, he sadly walked home.

The Dove Who Tried to Eat the Sun

— TU TALE —

LONG, long ago in another time, the raven was as white as snow, the owl worked and played by day, and the dove was the arrogant king of all the birds.

One day just before sunrise, as the dove was taking his peaceful morning stroll, he was suddenly interrupted by loud singing. He followed the blaring sound and soon came upon a flock of roosters. The boisterous roosters had gathered together to welcome the sun. Over and over they crowed their praises to the golden disk in the sky.

The jealous dove couldn't control his anger and shouted to the roosters, "Why are you singing to the sun? Don't you know I am king and you are my subjects?" The roosters kept singing. At last he turned his back on the flock and stormed off as the brilliant sun continued to rise in the east.

Shortly, he came upon a meadow filled with rainbow-colored flowers turning their smiling faces to greet the sun. The dove scolded the flowers: "Flowers, you have your own king. Why are you flattering the sun?"

The dove, now overcome with anger, stomped through the forest until he met a raven and an owl. He complained bitterly about the roosters and flowers saluting the sun. When he finished his story, the raven said, "Your Majesty, you are so right! That is insulting. Why don't you make a law so that nobody can honor the sun?"

The owl chimed in: "Your Highness, you have such a beautiful pair of wings. You can fly as far and wide as you like and destroy the sun."

"You are truly king," they both insisted. "You can surely kill the sun."

The dove, inspired by their words, was convinced they were right. "But how can the sun be destroyed?" he asked the raven and the owl.

"Majesty, I have a plan," the raven said, beckoning to them. "Please follow me home."

The raven led them to an enormous walnut tree in the middle of the forest. "Majesty, if we sew all the leaves together, we won't be able to see the sun," he said.

"Ha, ha, ha." The owl laughed so hard that he almost fell out of the tree. When he regained his balance, he went on: "How can a few leaves sewn together shut out the sun? They can only cover your house—not the sky."

"A stupid idea, very stupid," the dove shouted. With this the owl took the opportunity and said: "I have an idea. The sun looks to be no larger than a cake. Why don't we eat it?"

"That's a marvelous idea," the dove beamed. "Let's do it tomorrow."

Before dawn the next day the three began their flight to the sun. On and on they flew until the owl became too tired to continue. "I can't keep up with you," the owl said breathlessly, "I'll wait in the poplar tree. The dove and the raven were anxious to eat the sun and quickly said good-bye to the owl.

The dove and the raven had never flown so far and so fast. Over clouds and through a double rainbow they flew until they reached the sun. When they arrived at the sun's door, they broke it open and dashed inside while the sun was still fast asleep. Several times the dove tried to stab the sun with his pointed beak. Suddenly the sun jumped out of bed, and as his eyes opened, a stream of intense white light shot from his eyes and struck the dove. Before the dove had a chance to cry out, he was roasted.

The raven panicked when he saw what had happened to the dove. He tried to run away, but it was too late. His creamy white feathers were scorched charcoal black by the blazing heat of the sun.

The news about the dove and the raven soon reached the owl waiting in the tree. Frightened, he knew that he would be next. "What can I do? What can I do?" he shuddered. His only hope was to hide from the sun.

Since that time long, long ago, the owl hides in trees by day and only dares to come out at night. The formerly white raven now wears a blackened cloak of feathers. And the once arrogant dove has become the bird of peace.

The Tiger and the Bull

— DAI TALE —

IN ages past, on the southern border of Yunnan, near the Red River, stood two tall mountains. Once they were quite famous and the villagers called them Eastern Mountain and Western Mountain. On the top of Eastern Mountain lived a bull who considered himself to be king, and on the top of Western Mountain lived a tiger who also considered himself to be king. This did not pose a problem because the tiger and the bull stayed in their own territories and never bothered each other.

Then one day a hungry fox passed between the mountains and everything changed. The fox said, "If I could kill the tiger, I'd have food to last half a month. If I could kill the bull, I'd have food to last a month. Altogether, I wouldn't have to hunt for a very long time.

"But I'm only a fox. How can I kill a tiger and a bull?" He had almost dismissed his thought as being too foolish, when suddenly he had an idea. He headed toward Western Mountain.

As the fox approached the tiger, he remembered to kowtow. "Tiger King, just now as I passed by the Eastern Mountain, I overheard the bull cursing you. He swore that he would come to drive you out of your kingdom."

The tiger believed the lie and did not question the cunning fox. After he thanked the fox, he began to prepare for a fight.

The fox ran all the way to the Eastern Mountain. "I have brought you bad news," he gasped. Kneeling, he continued, "King Bull, I have just come from the Western Mountain. I heard the tiger cursing you. He declared that he would come to kill you and take your territory."

44

Hearing these words, the bull polished his horns and rushed down the mountain to fight the tiger.

When the bull and the tiger met at the bottom of the mountains, the tiger cried out, "Why do you want to drive me away?"

But the bull didn't hear clearly. He yelled back, "Did you really come to die?"

The tiger used his sharp teeth and the bull used his pointed horns to fight. They fought fiercely from morning until night. All the while the fox watched and laughed from behind a rock.

At the end of the duel both were so tired and so badly wounded that they fell to the ground and bled to death.

The shrewd fox had outsmarted the kings, and he had tiger meat and beef for his dinner.

The Ant and the Magpie

— MIAO TALE —

ONCE upon a time on a sweltering summer day, an ant worked the whole morning digging a tunnel. He dug until the afternoon sun shown straight overhead and he became very tired and very thirsty.

The weary ant walked to the pond for a refreshing drink. When he reached the edge of the pond, he climbed slowly up a blade of grass. As he approached the top of the blade, it began to bend toward the water. Just when he was about to take a drink, he lost his grip, and he fell into the water shouting, "Help, help!"

Directly above the drowning ant sat a magpie in a banyan tree. The kind bird saw what had happened and dropped a leaf into the pond. Shaking himself the soaked ant struggled up onto the leaf and paddled his way to the shore.

A few days later, as the ant was completing his tunnel, he heard a magpie singing in a tree overhead. At the same moment, right in his path, stood a hunter aiming a rifle at the bird.

Without thinking, the ant crawled up the hunter's leg and back and bit him on the side of his neck. The bite stung the hunter so badly that he missed his mark. The magpie flew safely away.

The following day the magpie met a fluffy gray squirrel sitting on the branch of a sycamore tree. "If it hadn't been for the ant, you wouldn't be here," squealed the squirrel. The magpie felt so grateful to the ant that he flew directly to the ant's home to thank him. "Thank you, my friend, for helping me," chirped the magpie.

"You are welcome," said the ant, "but you should remember that I also have to thank you for saving my life."

"We can all learn from this," said the gray squirrel. "We must live and work together in peace and harmony."

Why Snakes Bite Frogs

— MIAO TALE —

IN an ancient time, long ago, there was a famous snake that had a magnificent drum. Some even said it was magic.

One day a frog sitting on a lily pad heard the drum and admired the lucky snake for his possession. The frog wanted the drum for his own. He thought and thought, "How can I get the drum?"

Several days later the frog visited the snake's cottage. After inviting the frog inside and giving him a cup of jasmine tea, the polite snake asked, "What can I do for you, Mr. Frog?"

"My honored brother," he replied, "tomorrow I'm going to hold a memorial service for my ancestors, and I would like to use your marvelous drum. After the ceremony I will return it to you."

The snake did not hesitate. "Yes you can use the drum to honor your ancestors," he said. "To honor our ancestors is most important."

A few days went by and the snake wondered why the frog had not returned the drum. Finally, the snake couldn't wait any longer, and he went in search of his prized possession. The frog told him that the song of the drum had pleased his ancestors so much that he had played it day and night. "I couldn't offend my ancestors," he said. "I played it until it burst."

Since the drum was broken, there was no use saying anything that would embarrass the frog. The polite snake went on his way.

The snake missed his magical drum. He often thought he heard it as he walked in the forest. "My ears must be playing tricks," he said to himself.

Then one day the snake heard the beating of a drum far in the distance.

He followed the sound and soon came upon the frog playing his very own drum, the one the frog said was broken.

The frog continued to dance around, and pounding wildly on the drum, he didn't notice the snake right away. The angry snake hissed, "Why did you lie to me? Why didn't you return my drum?" Before the next words were out of his mouth, he lunged to bite the frog.

Since that day snakes continue to search for and kill dishonest frogs who might still be playing stolen drums.

The Dove and the Rooster

— YI TALE —

IN an earlier time, the dove and the rooster were best friends. They were such good friends that they decided to take a journey together. The pair walked almost a whole day from their village in the lowlands to the mountaintop. During their arduous trek they never came upon a drinking well. Their thirst persisted as they continued, but still there was no well in sight.

The dove finally said to the rooster, "We can't go on if we don't have water to drink." As he looked around at the rocky ground, he said, "We'll have to dig a well."

The rooster, surprised by what the dove had suggested, started shaking his head: "Oh, no. I'm certainly not going to dig a well."

The dove didn't mind working hard, and at once he began to dig. He dug and dug. All the while the rooster slept under a shady willow tree.

At last the well was complete. Water shot high into the sky like a broken string of pearls being slung into the air. The dove drank until he was satisfied and then sat back and closed his eyes.

The rooster was awakened by the spurting water. He leapt up and drank until he heard the dove shouting: "When I worked, you did nothing. You never gave me a hand, and now you are enjoying my efforts. It isn't fair! I'm sure the God of Thunder will punish you!"

The rooster felt guilty because he hadn't helped, and he was also scared, because the God of Thunder would surely come to punish him.

Since that day, when roosters drink, they lift their heads to look at the sky, still in fear that the God of Thunder will come to take revenge.

The Tiger and the Frog

— BOUYEI TALE —

HERE was once a majestic tiger who lived high up on the grassy steppe. Early one misty morning he went in search of water. He followed the well-worn path and came to a bubbling stream. As he took his first invigorating drink, the quiet was shattered by a noisy croaking frog. The uproarious sound continued and the tiger became curious. "Little one, how can you have such a loud voice?" he asked.

"Even though I have a small body, each day I eat a tiger for my meal," answered the frog. "So I have a booming voice."

This made the tiger angry. "Shut up!" he shouted. "If I hit you with my paw, I'll turn you into frog pie."

The frog appeared not to be frightened by the tiger's words and suggested they have a competition and see who would win. The tiger agreed.

The frog knew he could not beat the tiger, but he was too proud to break his word. He thought quickly and said, "Today I've been singing the whole morning and I'm tired. Let's compete tomorrow."

"Okay," the tiger agreed, and he left the frog sitting beside the stream.

After the tiger left, the frog began to worry. "Now I've really done it," he said to himself. "I was crazy to suggest such a thing."

Just as the frog was about to give up, along came an old peasant walking back to his village. The frog decided to ask him for help.

"I can give you one small piece of advice," the old peasant answered. "Hold on to his tail, hold on tight."

The next day the tiger and the frog met at the same place. The first con-

test was to see who could jump the highest. "On the count of three we'll both jump," said the frog.

One. Two. Before they got to three, the frog had jumped on the tiger's tail and held tight. On the count of three, the tiger jumped as high as he could, but the frog jumped higher from the tiger's tail and won.

This angered the tiger. "It doesn't count!" he shouted. "Let's see who can jump across the stream."

"That's fine with me," replied the frog.

Standing on the edge of the stream—one, two—but before they got to three, the frog had once again jumped on the tiger's tail. The tiger jumped as far as he could, but the frog jumped even farther from his tail. Again the frog won.

Embarrassed and frightened by losing, the tiger dashed away before he could become the frog's meal.

The frog was indebted to the peasant for his wise advice, and to repay him, the frog stayed in his field to catch bugs.

If you walk through the countryside tonight, you will still hear the grateful frog croaking his thanks. Listen carefully.

Wild Geese

— HUI TALE —

Y OU may have wondered about many things, but have you ever wondered why geese fly either in a straight line or in a "V" formation? Here is the reason.

Long ago a family of wild geese lived on a large lake in Xinjiang. During the day Grandfather Goose was in charge, and he led the entire family around the lake to play and look for food.

One day they played and worked especially hard, so that by the end of the day they were quite tired and sleepy. Grandfather Goose looked around to pick someone to stay awake and watch over the flock. Recently a hunter had tried to shoot some of the family members as they slept. They needed to be extremely careful.

That particular night the old goose chose his youngest grandson. "Tonight it is your turn to watch. Make sure you do not sleep. Listen carefully and watch attentively. If you notice anything unusual, flap your wings to wake the family."

The young goose said, "Grandpa, trust me. I will be careful. You go to sleep."

The old goose continued: "You are young. You have not experienced disaster. You can never be too careful."

The grandson was impatient. "Don't be tiresome, Grandpa. I know what to do."

At nightfall, in the misty rain, the young goose began his watch. Around midnight he began to feel cold and sleepy. Seeing everyone else asleep, he

thought it was unfair for him to have to stay awake and watch for the hunter in such bad weather.

He looked up at the sky and said, "The hunter will not come tonight. Anyway, it's almost dawn. There won't be any problem if I just shut my eyes for a few minutes." He closed his eyes and fell fast asleep.

The shrewd hunter knew the geese who watched the flock tended to fall asleep just before dawn. With his musket in his hand, he tiptoed close to the bushes where the family slept.

Soon the hunter located the geese. He quietly loaded his gun and aimed. Boom! Boom! Boom! The explosion broke the silence, and all the geese except for the grandfather were killed.

During the night Grandfather Goose had not slept deeply because he was worried. He had woken up just before the hunter fired. But it was too late to warn the others.

Whenever old Grandfather Goose met other geese, he told his sad story. Just because of one goose, the whole family was killed. "This is a painful lesson that we must always remember," he would say.

The wild geese learned from this tragedy and passed the story down from generation to generation. But just in case their children have forgetten the lesson, they always fly in a straight line, which stands for the Chinese character for "one" (—)—the one who didn't watch—or they fly in an upside down "V," which in Chinese stands for person (人)—the man with the gun.

Minority People of China

THE "MIDDLE KINGDOM," as China is known, is home to a population of over one billion three hundred million. Of these vast numbers 93 percent are Han (ethnic Chinese). The other 7 percent make up the fifty-five national minorities.

The sixty-seven million minority people, with few exceptions, live in remote border regions along the western reaches of China. The Han are located mainly in the densely populated eastern lowlands.

This book consists of Han stories as well as stories from twelve other minority nationalities. The Han tales were included because they are delightful, and they reflect the largest group in China with the oldest continuous culture in the world.

A short description of each minority group follows, in alphabetical order, to help the reader better understand these unique people.

■ Bouyei	▨ Miao	▨ Tu
▨ Dai	■ Mongolian	■ Yao
▨ Hani	■ Salar (Sala)	▨ Yi
▨ Hui	▨ Tibetan	▨ Zhuang

Minority Regions of China

THE BOUYEIS

The Bouyeis or, as they were called in ancient times, "Baiyue" were once scattered along the southern region of the Yangtze River. From their language, which belongs to the Zhuang-Dong group (a branch of the Sino-Tibetan language family), it can be shown that they were at one time closely related to the Zhuang minority. Over time the two groups separated, and their ancestors migrated to different parts of China.

The Bouyeis, who number over two million, are settled in Guizhou Province, mainly in the Qiannan and Anshun regions. A few thousand also have settled to the southwest in Yunnan Province.

Qiannan in Guizhou Province is the location of China's famous waterfall Huangguoshu. The unique geographical region, with magical limestone formations and deep caves, was formed by three rivers that intersect here.

The flowing rivers that formed the dramatic terrain also made the fertile plains and river valleys in which the Bouyeis grow wheat, maize, and sisal hemp. Close to the southern border of Guangxi, they can harvest two crops of rice a year.

Art is meaningful to the Bouyeis, and nature's marvelous designs can be seen in their colorful batiks. The procedure of painting on cloth with wax, dyeing the material, and removing the wax is an ancient art form that the Bouyeis have mastered.

A legends tells us that in ancient times a young girl learned to dye cloth red, blue, and green by using plants she found in the mountains. One day while she was working, a bee landed on her white cloth and left a small amount of wax. After she dyed the fabric, she saw that the spot that had wax on it was still white. From then on she began to experiment with the wax, producing many designs that are still in use today.

Bouyei women use the imaginatively designed batik material to fashion clothing. They are also skilled weavers and embroiderers. The edges of their clothes are embroidered with colorful flowers and geometric designs. Their multilayered fashions are works of art. At one time the women wound long strips of cloth around their heads to make turbans, but now they use towels purchased from the department store.

Folk music is another art form that has been highly developed by the Bouyeis. During the "Bull Holiday" in spring, bronze drums decorated with frogs and other mythical creatures are beaten wildly as dancing and singing continue for six days.

The Bouyeis, unlike the Han, are not at all bashful about showing their fondness for the opposite sex. This bold display of affection is heard in the antiphonal singing among the young men and women. If a man is interested in a woman, he sends her a gift of indigo dye. The person who delivers the gift sings a verse to let her know who sent it. If the woman is not interested, she politely declines with a song, but if she is interested, she smiles in agreement and the lovers go off together. Antiphonal singing is important for courtship and for all festivals.

THE DAIS

The Dai population totals almost one million, divided into four main branches: the Sui Dai, Han Dai, Huayao Dai, and Kemu. These groups live mainly in two sections of Yunnan Province, Dehong and Xishuangbanna. These subtropical regions have fertile soil and plentiful rainfall that make for an agricultural abundance. The Dais are experienced farmers, who farmed with oxen and elephants as early as the eighth century. Sugar, coffee, mangoes, pineapple, bananas, hemp, rubber, and the world-famous Pu'er tea are grown by the Dais.

Traditional Dai houses are made of wood and bamboo and built on stilts. The upper story is occupied by the family; the lower provides storage and is used for cattle. The balconies around the house and the pointed thatched roof allow a free flow of air to circulate through the dwelling and keep it cool. Changes are taking place throughout the countryside, however, and many of the traditional wooden houses are being replaced by brick structures.

The Dais have a rich and colorful culture, and the people are strongly influenced by Buddhism. Their religion plays a part in daily life and is reflected in poetry, painting, sculpture, and in ornately decorated temples dispersed throughout the villages. In Xishuangbanna it is still common to send young boys to the temple to learn to read and write. Only a few stay to become monks, while most return to secular life.

The Dai language was said to belong to the Zhuang-Dong branch of the Sino-Tibetan language family. But recently linguists have questioned the derivation of the Dai language and think it has its own branch.

In cities and villages Dai as well as the Han language is in daily use. The marketplace is filled with conversations, information is broadcasted on loudspeakers, news coverage is heard on the radio in the two languages.

The Dais in the southwestern section of China have their own written script, which is alphabetic and derived from Indian. Many books have been translated from Chinese into Dai. Magazines and newspapers written in Dai can also be found in Dehong and Xishuangbanna.

Another form of communication is singing and dancing. These are an important part of the Dai daily life. Young children in villages practice songs and imitate the adult dancers. The "Peacock Dance," with its graceful and intricate movements, is one of the most beautiful and most difficult to perform. Attention to movement can also be seen in the charming manner in which the Dai women carry themselves.

The Dai women's grace is enhanced by their traditional dress. Their willowy figures are clothed in tight, long-sleeved blouses with colorful patterned sarongs. A silver belt wound around their slender waists keeps the sarong in place. Clothing and hair style can be a clue to which branch of Dai they belong to.

Festivals are good places to observe the Dais. For the Dais the most important festival is the "Water Splashing Festival," held during the Dai New Year, which is in mid-April. Everyone gets wet. The story goes:

> Long, long ago a demon-king captured seven beautiful Dai women for his harem. The women wanted to return to their families, but to do so they had to kill the demon-king. The only way they could kill him was to choke him with his own hair. When his head fell to the ground, it exploded into fire. They had to hold it so that the fire would not spread. As they held the head, people splashed water to cool themselves and to wash away the dirt and blood. Still to this day people pour, splash, and sometimes drench each other to receive the New Year's blessing.

THE HANIS

The Hanis are said to be descendants of the Qiangs, who lived in the secluded Qinghai-Tibet Plateau centuries ago. It is believed that the Hanis were at one time closely related to the Yis and Lahus. During historical times the Hanis migrated to the provinces of Sichuan and Yunnan and settled on the level mountaintops.

Their high terraced farms stretch for miles in all directions, and the many tiers make the mountains appear to be sculptured works of art. On these steep slopes they grow rice, sugar, cotton, peanuts, and tea. The surrounding mountains also yield medicinal herbs that are useful to the Hanis as well as to the outside world.

The Hani women like jewelry, and few can be seen without earrings, bracelets, and necklaces. Their dress is usually a dark cotton robe worn over long pants. The edges of the garments are decorated with brilliant embroidery and bright yarn tassels. At one time pieces of silver and jade adorned the close-fitting hats of the Hani women, but recently the "silver" ornaments are fashioned out of scrap metal or from the caps of soda bottles. The men do not dress as elaborately. They dress much as the Hans, but a few still wear the traditional turbans.

The Hanis celebrate many festivals that are centered on planting and harvesting. The biggest celebration is the "Tenth Moon Festival" that begins the Hani New Year. The village elder, a man, presides over the festival. He tastes all the food prepared by the women prior to the banquet. Then the male heads of each family can take their seats around the table, and eating and drinking begins. Younger men serve wine and bring more dishes, while the women, who have eaten earlier, sit in a circle and softly sing.

THE HUIS

The Huis, also known as Moslems, have a population of eight million. The Huis live in all parts of China, but the largest communities are in the provinces of Xinjiang, Qinghai, Gansu, Hunan, and Yunnan.

During the seventh century many Arab and Persian merchants followed the "Silk Road" to trade in China. As time passed, more and more came, and they introduced the Islamic faith. The group that adopted the Islamic religion became the Huis. The Chinese character for "Hui" also means "return" or "go back." Maybe these people had, at one time, planned on returning to an earlier home. Now they cannot easily be distinguished from the Han, because they are not a separate ethnic group, but rather a religious minority.

The Huis adhere to the religious practices of Islam, which include reading from the Koran, praying to Mecca, visiting the mosque on Fridays and holy days, and abstaining from eating pork or drinking alcohol.

The Huis celebrate Han festivals as well as Ramadan and the birth of Mohammed. Very few of the Huis are able to make the pilgrimage to Mecca.

THE MIAOS

With a population of over five and a half million, the Miao ethnic group is one of the largest in southwest China. Most reside in Guizhou; others are spread throughout Yunnan, Hunan, Sichuan, and Guangxi provinces.

Spoken Miao is still in use today. Three main Miao dialects are used, and they are quite different from each other. According to legend, long ago the Miaos had a written language, but it was lost when they crossed a large river. Currently many Miaos use Chinese as a common language.

The Miaos are one of the oldest nationalities, with a history of over four thousand years. Their traditions include a love for singing, especially love songs, and dancing. Both are popular among young and old alike. At festivals they often hold song and dance contests.

The Miaos have many fascinating legends, but the one about the disappearance of the sun is especially interesting. As the story goes:

> Clouds and mist covered a village for so long that crops did not grow, people became sick, and the animals began to die. An old man in the village came up with a solution. He suggested that everyone in the village make a musical instrument *(lusheng)* and blow it at the same time. For three days and nights the people danced and blew their pipes. The sun returned.

A Miao New Year would not be complete without the sound of the *lusheng,* a musical instrument made of bamboo pipes of varying lengths. The *lusheng* is still used to dispel the clouds and bring out the sun.

The Miaos excel at batik, embroidery, and cross-stitch. Most Miao girls learn these arts at an early age. The designs they use include dragons, flowers, birds, insects, and geometric patterns that reflect a love for nature and their environment. Miao handicrafts are sold in China and abroad.

THE MONGOLS

The Mongols have a long history and tradition. Formerly a nomadic people scattered along the Ergun River during the seventh century, they later moved to the northern grasslands of western Mongolia. In the early thirteenth century Genghis Khan's army fought and conquered the surrounding tribes and united them.

With the unification a written script for the Mongolian language was developed. The Mongolian language is part of the Altaic language family and has three dialects: Inner Mongolian, Barag-Buryat, and Uirad. In the thirteenth century the *Inside History of Mongolia* was compiled. This literary and historical work recording the nomadic life of the Mongols shows that very early they had already achieved high levels in agriculture, handicrafts, hunting, and religion.

The Mongols, with their population of more than three million, live in Inner Mongolia, Jilin, Heilongjiang, Qinghai, and Xinjiang. They have a distinctive way of life that stems from their earlier nomadic ways and their herding economy. Their diet includes mutton, beef, and dairy products along with millet, grains, and vegetables. They drink a tea made with milk, butter, and salt. Their houses, or yurts, as they are called, are unique to the Mongols. A yurt is a tentlike portable dwelling made of hides or felt that can be dismantled and carried long distances.

In July during Nadam Festival (*nadam* means "games" in Mongolian), the yurts are moved to Hohhot, the capital of Inner Mongolia. Growing up on horseback, Mongols are skilled riders. Their games and festivals include competition on horseback, archery, and wrestling.

Religion still plays a meaningful role in their lives, but it has changed from the earlier shamanism to include Lamaism, an order of Buddhism.

THE SALAS (OR SALARS)

Most of the seventy thousand Salas live in Qinghai and Gansu provinces. Their origins are obscure, but legends say that they came from Samarkand in Central Asia as early as 200 B.C. They came to trade jewelry and spices for Chinese silk. Over the years they intermarried with the Huis, Tibetans, and Hans, and their original Turkic language has now come to include many new words from these associations.

The Sala economy is based on farming, lumber, and animal husbandry. The Salas grow barley, wheat, and potatoes, and many families have apple and walnut orchards.

Salas are devout Moslems, and they are deeply influenced by Islam. In keeping with their religion, Sala men often wear flat-topped brimless hats in either black or white, and Sala women wear scarves on their heads.

THE TIBETANS

"The Roof of the World," as Tibet is known, houses most of the Tibetan people, but many are dispersed throughout Qinghai, Gansu, Yunnan, and Sichuan provinces for a total population of about four million.

Tibet is situated between the two great civilizations of India and China, and both have been influential. India probably had the earlier influence, especially concerning religion. Chinese contact can be dated from the early seventh century (Tang dynasty), when King Songzan Gampo married a Han princess, Wen Cheng, to cement ties between their countries.

The Tibetans have an ancient and rich heritage including a language (of the Sino-Tibetan language family) and a written script. Their literature includes the longest epic poem in the world, "Khan Gesar," which began as an oral tale of how a hero purged the people of sin. The epic gives a historical account of ancient times in Tibet. Many other early Tibetan texts give information about language, philosophy, mathematics, religion, medicine, and architecture.

Tibetan architecture has a distinctive style that is reflected in the Portala Palace which stands atop a mountain in Lhasa. The impressive monument rises naturally with the slope of the land, and its golden roofs glimmer in the sunlight. An imposing masterpiece, it is a tribute to Tibetan architecture and the Tibetan people.

The richness of the Tibetan people contrasts sharply with the barrenness of Tibet's land. The starkness of the landscape and the long, cold winters make it a wonder that anything can grow. Hardy wheat does manage to grow year round, and barley and peas, which grow quickly during the summer, are the main crops. *Zamba,* a roasted barley or pea flour mixed with tea, is a food staple. The shaggy yak supplies the Tibetans with milk, butter, wool, hides, and transportation.

Tibetan men wear long fur or felt robes with long pants. While working, they often leave one arm exposed. Women wear long robes with skirts underneath and tie rainbow-colored aprons around their waists. Colored silk strands are woven into their braided black hair. Both men and women wear hats and boots made from either felt or fur. Tibetans like decorations and wear heavy silver jewelry set with turquoise or other colorful stones around their necks, wrists, and fingers. The Tibetans are dazzling to behold twirling their prayer wheels as they circumambulate the temples clockwise.

THE TUS

The Tus call themselves "Qagan," which means "white Mongol." Their language, which has no written script, is similar to the Mongolian branch of the Altaic family. For writing the Tus use Chinese characters. They have adopted many religious terms from the Tibetans and commonly use words borrowed from the Hans. They claim that their ancestor was a Mongol general who fought under Genghis Khan. General Gerelt (Gerelite) is worshiped to this day, and a bronze statue in his honor stands in the Youning Lamasery in Huzhu. Historical records confirm that Genghis Khan did send an army to this part of the world.

The Tus number about one hundred sixty thousand. Over the centuries they have changed their way of life from herding goats and sheep to farming. They live mainly in Qinghai and Gansu in arid, hilly, inaccessible regions. With painstaking efforts the Tus have cultivated the difficult land.

Even though life is hard for the Tus, they have developed a love of art. Their intricately embroidered clothing includes jackets, shoes, socks, belts, and hats with imaginative floral designs in bright primary colors.

THE YAOS

Known as "hill people," the Yaos number around one and a half million and live mainly in Guangxi, Hunan, Yunnan, and Guangdong on the mountain peaks. The Yaos are a proud people who chose to withdraw into remote areas instead of submitting to the corvée labor system imposed on them by earlier rulers of China.

At one time the Yaos were hunters, but later they turned to slash-and-burn agriculture. They burned the forested hillsides and planted seeds in the warm ashes. The ashes acted as fertilizer, and several crops could be harvested before they had to move on. With this lifestyle they were unable to settle down for any length of time. They had little need for permanent dwellings in the isolated areas, so they made makeshift houses out of wood and bamboo.

Forestry is now an important part of the Yao economy. Timber is grown on the steep hillsides and is harvested as one of their cash crops. Often trees are planted in rows with vegetable gardens growing in between the rows. Many Yaos stay in villages and do an intensive form of farming known as garden agriculture. Their staple crops are rice, millet, beans, sweet potatoes, and taro. Commonly grown vegetables include peppers, soybeans, and pumpkins. Medicinal herbs, mushrooms, star anise, and textiles also add to their incomes.

The Yaos are clearly related to the Miaos, as can be seen in their similar languages. The Miao-Yao language belongs to a branch of the Sino-Tibetan family. At an earlier time the Yaos did not have a written language and kept records by carving notches on wood or bamboo; now they use Chinese characters.

Like the Miaos, the Yaos are especially talented in producing batik, brocade, and embroidery. Their multicolored attire can be seen on both males and females. Yao women like to decorate themselves with heavy silver jewelry and can be seen displaying it in the marketplace.

The Yaos celebrate "Spring Festival" (New Year's according to the lunar calendar) by shooting off firecrackers to scare away the evil spirits. They gather together for a family banquet on the holiday eve, but the following day is set aside for young men and women to get together outside the village to sing, dance, and participate in sports competition.

THE YIS

With a population of over five and a half million, the Yis are the largest minority group in southwestern China. They are scattered over the provinces of Yunnan, Sichuan, Guizhou, and Guangxi. The Yis tend to live mainly in mountainous regions.

The Yi minority group is very large, because it is made up of several other ethnic groups that also lived in the same areas. These groups were included in the Yi
population count by mistake. The confusion came because a collective term,
"lolo," was used that labeled all the minorities together. This derogatory term in
Chinese means southern barbarian ethnic group. The Chinese characters for *lolo*
use the animal radical instead of the person radical. It shows that these "lolo"
were not considered human. Because the "lolo" were incorrectly counted together,
the name covers more than the original Yis. It is no wonder that the "Yi" customs,
dress, and language differ greatly from place to place.

Traditionally the Yis have been a sophisticated group with a spoken language
and a written script. The Yi language is Tibeto-Burman, a language group of the
Sino-Tibetan language family. The old Yi language was compiled during the thirteenth century and consisted of about ten thousand words. Old Yi script can still
be seen carved on stone tablets in many areas.

With the Yi people's long history has come a culture that includes folk literature, poetry, tales, fables, proverbs, and epic stories. One of the well-known epics
is "Ashima." This love story has been translated into English and was made into a
movie in China. Sometimes it is performed as a play at the "Stone Forest" outside
of Kunming in Yunnan.

Early the Yis developed a solar calendar divided into ten months of thirty-six
days each that was widely used until just recently. This calendar still marks their
holidays.

During the sixth solar month of their calendar, the annual "Torch Festival" is
held. The Yis celebrate the harvest by lighting torches and encircling the fields to
frighten away insects. This practice ensures the Yis a good harvest for their potatoes, corn, buckwheat, and other crops. The celebration includes singing and
dancing and horseback, wrestling, and archery competition.

THE ZHUANGS

The Zhuang minority, with the largest population of any of the minorities, numbers over thirteen million people. They inhabit Guangxi, Guangdong, and Yunnan provinces.

Linguists are studying the Zhuang language and the derivation is still debat-
able. Many still believe the language belongs to the Zhuang-Dong branch of Sino-
Tibetan.

In ancient times the Zhuang did have a written script, but they later borrowed
Chinese characters. Recently a writing system for Zhuang was developed based
on the Latin alphabet. This Romanized script is now used for writing the Zhuang

language. The Zhuangs have lived in southern China for centuries, mixing closely with the Hans. Even though they identify closely with the Hans, the Zhuangs still maintain some of their special festivals. The "Devil Festival," which comes each year in August, is celebrated by offering food and sticky rice to ancestors and ghosts.

Another aspect of traditional Zhuang culture is antiphonal singing, especially during courtship. Young men and women still gather to sing folk songs. They taunt and echo each other in playful songs, which sometimes become quite bawdy. Laughing and encouragement come from listeners and onlookers. This singing still goes on in villages as well as in big city parks.

Being in the south, the Zhuangs have a mild climate and usually enough rainfall to harvest two or three crops of rice a year. Their other crops include corn, sweet potatoes, sugarcane, bananas, litchis, and pineapples.

As early as the tenth century, Guangxi was known as an important silkworm-breeding area. Zhuang women learned many techniques from Sichuan brocaders and then developed their own traditional brocade designs, which include animals, birds, fish, and flowers. Zhuang brocade was famous in China during the Ming and Qing dynasties and has not lost its artistic appeal in the modern world.

About the Authors

CAROLYN HAN received a B.A. in English from the University of Hawaii at Hilo and an M.A. in comparative literature from San Diego State University. She has taught at Hawaii Community College, where she was awarded Lecturer of the Year in 1991–1992, and at Hawaii Preparatory Academy.

During three years of living in Sichuan and Yunnan provinces in the People's Republic of China, Ms. Han taught English to university students from approximately twenty-two different ethnic backgrounds. This gave her the opportunity to know these colorful people and begin collecting their folktales.

JAY HAN was educated at Yunnan Teacher's College in Kunming, the People's Republic of China. He has taught English and is currently working in private industry.

(Left to right):
Li Ji, Carolyn Han, Jay Han.
(Photo by Carol Soderlund)

About the Artist

LI JI received a degree from the Sichuan Art Institute and studied at the Beijing Central Art Institute. He is a lecturer in art and specializes in wood-block printing at Yunnan Art Institute. He has broad firsthand knowledge of the minority peoples of the People's Republic of China, and he possesses a deep understanding and love for animals and the environment.

Production Notes

Composition and paging were done on the
Quadex Composing System and typesetting
on the Compugraphic 8400 by the design
and production staff of University of
Hawaii Press.

The text typeface is Sabon and the display
typeface is Compugraphic Metropolis.

Offset presswork and binding were done by
Tien Wah Press (Pte.) Ltd. Text paper is
150gsm Artic Matte.